Speech Class Rules

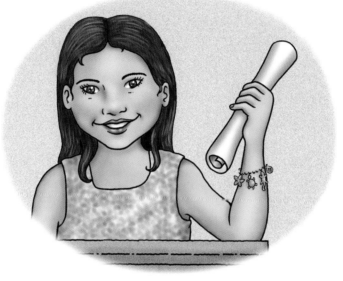

The Speech Place Publishing, an RKR Ventures LLC Company

For my guys ~ Kevin, Shane, & Kyle.
And for my Dad.
–RMW

For my wonderful grown-up kids, Alex and Jessica.
–LB

Acknowledgements:

Thank you to all of the dedicated professionals with whom I've had the pleasure of working ~ most especially: Teale Lee, Emi Isaki, Claudia Canady, Claudia Kikuta, Betty Menking and Dorlas Riley.

Thank you to all "my kids" and their supportive families who inspire me on a daily basis.

Thank you to Lou & Loel for making this project such a pleasure.

Thank you to Bonny Becker for sharing your expertise.

Ronda M. Wojcicki

Text ©2007 by Ronda M. Wojcicki • Illustrations ©2007 by Loel Barr
Book and cover design by Lou M. Pollack

All rights reserved. No part of this publication may be reproduced, stored in a retrieval system, or transmitted in any form, or by any means, electronic, mechanical, photocopying, recording, or otherwise, without written permission of the publisher and/or illustrator. For information regarding permissions, please contact The Speech Place Publishing through our website at www.TheSpeechPlace.com or e-mail CS@TheSpeechPlace.com

To order additional copies, visit www.TheSpeechPlace.com

The Speech Place Publishing, an RKR Ventures LLC Company
1810-A York Road #432
Lutherville, MD 21093

Printed in the U.S.A. by Worzalla

ISBN-978-0-9794102-0-8
Library of Congress Control Number: 2007903039
First Edition, 2007

The Speech Place Publishing

Today is a special day.
The gym is bursting with balloons!

Ceremony begins at 2:00

Today is not just any day.
Today is speech graduation, and I,
Laney Lynn, am graduating from
speech class!

I borrowed my cousin Kiana's gecko charm for good luck.

I practiced walking across the stage.

My parents and my aunt said they would sit near the front so I could see them.

What if I trip going up the stairs and my skirt goes over my head and everyone sees my underwear?

What if I forget my notecard and I can't remember what I wrote, so I have to say the Pledge of Allegience? (it's the only thing I know by heart!)

GIRLS

What if I have to use the bathroom right before my name is called and I miss the whole thing?

The only thing scarier than this was my first day of speech class. I remember how I didn't want to go because I was the only one from Mrs. Read's class.

I remember raising my hand in class. When it was my turn to answer, sometimes I'd use the wrong word or mix up the words in my sentence. Mrs. Read told me that Miss W. might be able to help. That's when I met Felipe, Andrew, Paige and Vanessa.
We all became a speech group.

Speech class is fun, but it's not easy. Miss W. has a poster in our speech room with a list of **Speech Class Rules.**

Everybody works on different stuff in speech class. Miss W. calls it your "goals".

The last goal that I worked on is called sequencing. That was my favorite one because I got to play games and put scrambled up pictures in order. And then I got to tell the group a story about them!

When Felipe started coming to speech class, he talked with a lot of "bumps". (That's what Miss W. calls it when he stops in the middle of a word or sentence, or he repeats something). She says that some people call it stuttering.

But now he's learning to use "easy speech" with soft starts and lots of breaths. Sometimes when we are having lots of fun, Felipe forgets and starts to talk really fast.

Miss W. points to the poster and says, "Remember, **Speech Class Rules**".

We all say "#1. We speak slowly and clearly", and she just smiles.

Paige doesn't like to talk a lot. Her speech goals are to start up conversations and then keep them going.

Miss W. says I'm a great practice partner for her because I have so many ideas to share.

But sometimes, I have SO many ideas that Paige doesn't get much of a chance.

That's when Miss W. points to the poster and says, "Remember, **Speech Class Rules**"...

"#2", we chant. "We take turns talking!"

And Miss W. smiles.

Before I met Vanessa in speech class, I thought she always had a sore throat. It turns out she has tiny bumps in her throat called nodules from yelling too much and talking too loudly. I didn't know there was anyone who talked more than me!

Vanessa's working on gentle speech and good vocal hygiene, like drinking lots of water and getting enough rest. Instead of shouting above the class, she learns to raise her hand and wait. She even wears a special whistle on the  playground that Miss W. gave her, so she can call people without shouting when she's far away. But every once in a while, she forgets and yells. Miss W. points to the poster and says, "Remember, **Speech Class Rules**". Vanessa reads, "#3. We use soft voices".

And Miss W. smiles.

Andrew works on speech sounds like
's' and 'r' and 'ch'. Miss W. calls this
articulation. I think that's a pretty long
word for all those little sounds.

Andrew gets to use Miss W.'s giant mirror
and her wacky feather. When he makes his
's' sounds, we all remind him that only the
middle of the feather can move. That's how
he learns to control the air. It's pretty cool.

Miss W. says it's extra important for Andrew to do his homework because he needs to practice his sounds over and over.

SPEECH CLASS RULES
1. We speak slowly and clearly.
2. We take turns talkin
3. We use soft voices.
4. We do our homewor
5. We respec each oth
e have

So it drives Miss W. batty when Andrew forgets to do his homework. She shakes her head and points to the poster and says, "Remember, **Speech Class Rules**". "I know", Andrew sighs, "# 4. We do our homework". Then she smiles.

Now that I'm finished with all of my speech goals, I'm graduating from speech class. I'm really going to miss my friends in my speech group and all the fun we have.

I know Miss W. will just smile.

QUESTIONS FOR THE CLASSROOM:

1 Laney Lynn and her friends went to speech class to get extra help with their speech and language skills. Lots of children get extra help with different skills.

Have you ever received extra help for anything?

If so, tell the class about your experience.

2 Does anyone here go to speech class?

How is your speech class different from Laney Lynn's?

How is it the same?

What is your favorite part about speech class?
(Give everyone who is in speech class a chance to share with the group.)

3 Is there anyone who used to go to speech class, but graduated like Laney Lynn?

When did you go to speech class?

What did you work on there?

Did you do or earn anything special when you finished?

▸ For children who answered Numbers 2 & 3:

What would you like your classmates to know about speech class?

4 For all:

Do you think that Speech Class Graduation is a good idea?

Why or why not?

5 Does anyone know the name of the *Speech-Language Pathologist, Speech Therapist* or *Speech Teacher* (choose appropriate title) at our school?

Where is his/her office?

QUESTIONS FOR HOME:

1 Do you, or does anyone you know, go to speech class? If yes,

How is it different from Laney Lynn's speech class?

How is it the same?

If you attend speech class, what is your favorite part?

If you know someone else who attends speech class, ask them to tell you about their experience.

2 Why do you think Laney Lynn was afraid to go to speech class for the first time?

3 What have you done that was scary the first time? How did you feel after you did it?

FOR CHILDREN ABOUT TO BEGIN SPEECH THERAPY:

4 Have you met the *Speech-Language Pathologist, Speech Therapist, Speech Teacher* (choose appropriate title) at your school?

5 Perhaps before your speech class begins, your teacher could bring you to meet the *Speech-Language Pathologist, Speech Therapist, Speech Teacher* (choose appropriate title) and you could ask any questions that you might have. What would you want to ask?

NOTE TO PARENTS:

According to the American Speech-Language-Hearing Association (ASHA), communication disorders are among the most common disabilities in the United States. The most recent statistics from the United States Department of Education report that in the Fall of 2002 alone, more than 6.5 million children with disabilities between the ages of 3-21 received special education services in the public schools. Approximately 22% of these children received services for speech or language disorders as a primary diagnosis. Many more received services for speech/language impairments secondary to other conditions. These numbers do not include speech/language services rendered outside public schools – in private schools, private practice, community clinics, rehabilitation centers, hospitals, colleges and universities.

Research shows that early intervention of communication disorders paired with subsequent intervention can greatly improve a child's overall future and success!*

If you have concerns about your child's speech or language development, discuss them with your child's teacher and pediatrician to determine if an evaluation by a Speech-Language Pathologist is appropriate.

*VanDyke, D.C., & Holte, L. (2003, July). Communication disorders in children. *Pediatric Annals, 32(7):* 436.

PRODUCTION NOTES:

This book was typeset primarily in Officina Bold. Illustrations were first sketched by hand, then refined and finished in color with the computer.

About the Illustrator:
Loel Barr is a freelance illustrator and painter who has illustrated for numerous books, magazines, newpapers, collateral and advertising media. She exhibits her work in upstate New York's Hudson Valley, where she recently relocated from Washington DC.

About the Designer:
Lou M. Pollack is a book and graphic designer, illustrator, fine artist and teacher of creative expression who also loves exploring her passion for dance, music and rythym and working with the healing power of art. She has a BFA from Parsons/The New School.